JULIO

SEPTIEMBRE

NOVIEMBRE

AGOSTO

OCTUBRE

DICIEMBRE

¡FiESTA!

A Celebration of
Latino Festivals

Sherry Shahan

Illustrated by
Paula Barragán

AUGUST HOUSE
Little folk
ATLANTA

Published 2009 by August House LittleFolk
3500 Piedmont Road NE, Suite 310, Atlanta, Georgia 30305,
404–442–4420
http://www.augusthouse.com

Manufactured in Korea

10 9 8 7 6 5 4 3 2 1

LIBRARY OF CONGRESS CATALOGING-IN-PUBLICATION DATA

Shahan, Sherry.
    Fiesta! : a celebration of latino festivals / Sherry Shahan ;
illustrated by Paula Barragán.
        p.   cm.
    ISBN 978-0-87483-861-9 (alk. paper)
    1. Festivals—Latin America—Juvenile literature. 2. Latin America—
Social life and customs—Juvenile literature. I. Barragán, Paula, 1963–
II. Title.

GT4813.5.S43   2009
394.2698—dc22

                                    2008001462

The paper used in this publication meets the minimum requirements of
the American National Standard for Information Sciences—Permanence
of Paper for Printed Library Materials,
ANSI Z39.48–1984.

AUGUST HOUSE   PUBLISHERS   ATLANTA

For the biggest celebration of all,
Cooper Alan
—SS

Para mis guaguas,
Manuela y Jacinto xo
—PB

Fiesta de San Antonio Abad

Polka-dot cows stride
beside candy-striped burros.

Baby chicks bob and chirp
under itty-bitty smocks.

The village sways in song:
Moo and cock-a-doodle-do!

JANUARY

ENERO

January 17th is the day of St. Anthony. In small Mexican villages, children parade their pets down dirt roads to a church to be blessed. A child may carry a puppy dressed up in satin pants or a kitten in a hoop skirt. Soon the churchyard is a caterwaul of neighs, moos, yelps, quacks, cackles, chirps, barks, and snorts. Meanwhile, a priest stands atop a stone wall, cradling a vessel. As the children and animals pass beneath him, he sprinkles them with holy water.

Wine Harvest

Singing rises from vines.
Barefoot workers press grapes,
marching time:

Squish-squash-slosh

Barrels swell with fruity juice.

FEBRUARY

FEBRERO

The sun winks over the horizon as workers line up in vineyards. They pose straight and tall, pretending to be soldiers. The farm owner impersonates a high-ranking general.

The barefoot workers crush grapes, all stomping to the rhythm of drums. If someone slows at his task, the general playfully tosses him aside. Laughter follows the mock punishment, along with a soothing sip from the barrel.

Later, the workers capture the general and poke flowers into his clothes. He barters for his release by giving up a barrel of his finest wine. Music and old-time songs stream from the grand *hacienda*. This time workers kick up their grape-stained feet in dance.

Corn-Planting Ceremony

Candles flicker and flare,
lighting tilled fields.

Golden drops shower down.
Good luck!

Seeds slip beneath the soil,
awaiting spring rains.

MARCH

MARZO

The night before planting corn kernels, participants light incense in harrowed fields and sprinkle the ground with home-brewed brandy. Once the sun rises, women set down burning candles in the direction of the four winds. By honoring soil and seeds, the celebrants believe, they will help the cornstalks mature with strength.

A rich harvest ensures corn dishes on every table at every meal. Corn scratch feeds chickens and pigs. Corn husks thatch huts.

Sealing the Frost

A cliff-hanger clings to a rope
beside an icy crack.

Plaster is smoothed over rock,
sealing in a killing frost,
saving baby crops.

APRIL

High in certain mountains, rain falls into rocky crevices where it freezes. People of tradition believe these cracks must be sealed. Otherwise young shoots of corn may suffer frostbite. A prayer-maker with special powers over the weather guides a procession up a mountain trail. Gradually, he is lowered by rope over the edge of a cliff where he dangles beside a frost crack. After plugging the opening, he trudges back to the village, trailed by grateful townspeople.

ABRIL

Cinco de Mayo

A play is staged on this day:

Cannons shoot.
Bugles blare.

Armies fight
hand-to-hand.

Actors shout,
"¡Viva México!"

On the fifth day of May, Mexican celebrants reenact the victory of Mexico over the French army in 1862. A mock battle between Mexican and French troops rages long after sunset. Earsplitting cannonshots shatter the air, and actors shout lines they've learned by heart from one side to the other. Dolls bounce on the backs of female soldiers. Bugles signal orders.

Finally, the French flag is taken down. Fallen soldiers from both armies are respectfully laid out on stretchers. Soon each man is carted off to the somber tune of a funeral march.

MAYo

Inti Raymi

Flowers bloom
on plains,
hillsides,
wild and yellow.

Kettles spill spicy smells,
sweet and sour:

Cinnamon sticks,
simmering quince,
poaching fish.

JUNE

During the winter solstice the sun is farthest from the earth. In ancient times, Incan farmers feared the life-giving rays might disappear forever. To honor Inti, the Sun God, worshippers sweep the streets free of evil spirits. Masked men dance to throbbing drums and tooting flutes. Plumed troupes lead llamas to the main square, where one is sacrificed. The offering is believed to lure the sun back and warm the earth. Afterwards, crowds feast on traditional dishes, such as *mazamorra*. Once again, a new year has begun.

JUNIO

JULY

Pilgrimage of Saut d'Eau

People cross streams
on wobbly logs.
Pebbles crunch beneath bare feet.

All kneel by a waterfall

Towering
Tumbling
Stumbling

JULIO

This pilgrimage passes villages along a dirt road as it meanders to a spring-fed pool. Misty spray rises, and sunlight squints over volcanic cliffs. It was once believed that mysterious spirits dwelled here.

One of the bathers in the pool suddenly lapses into a trance and utters senseless words. The others recognize him as a serpent spirit and lead him to shore. There they crowd in to ask favors large and small. Later, the spirit person naps beneath a huge fig tree.

Before journeying home, travelers tie colorful cords around the tree as offerings. They pinch bits of sacred earth and press them into small squares of cloth.

Pilgrimage to Nuestra Señora de los Angeles Basilica

Behind the church
bubbles a fountain,
special spring water.

Come now, dear friends,

Drink it.
Bathe in it.

Bottle up wishes.

AUGUST

AGOSTO

Once upon an ancient time, a young girl was out gathering firewood. She happened upon a stone statue lying near a pond, glowing with an unearthly light. She wrapped the treasure with care in her tattered shawl and later hid it in her hut.

By dawn, as the legend goes, it had disappeared. She wandered to the same pool the following morning and found the statue again. Once again, she tucked it away for safekeeping. And again, it disappeared.

The girl's tale trickled from friend to friend, then to the village priest. Recognizing the shimmering statue as a miracle, he arranged for a shrine to be erected on the site. To this day, a pilgrimage winds its way to the sanctuary along a route strewn with bright-colored flowers and sandy stripes.

Águas de Oxalá

Clanging gongs
Throbbing drums

Raspy chants

Rat-a-tat-pitter-pat

Young women whirl in white,
performing stories of new life.

SEPTEMBER

SEPTIEMBRE

All is dark and unusually silent in the middle of this night. If one is very still, a tiny bell may be heard, tinkling in the shadows. Then, as silently as ghosts, men and women shuffle out into the open. Each person totes an earthen pot. Taking turns, they kneel at a hallowed stream and fill them.

A wooden hut sits on a hilltop. It holds a receptacle for the sacred water. By daybreak, the last person has emptied his pot, thus completing the ancient ritual. Soon, music and dancing erupt outside the hut. It continues on and on until daughters of the saint sink into a hypnotic trance.

Fiesta de
San Francisco de Asís

A man carries a chicken
in one hand.

With the other,
he twirls a girl
around a bottle.

Onlookers cheer,

"Careful, now, not to knock
the silver coin off the stopper!"

Tricky feet tie and untie knots
never missing a heel-toe beat.

OCTOBER

OCTUBRE

Many centuries ago, a young man named Francis listened to a beggar's plea. He emptied his pockets and generously shared the contents. His friends laughed and teased him for such foolishness. That night, his father scolded him.

Sometime later, Francis resolved to give up his life of sport and merriment. Yet again, his friends chided him. When they laughingly asked if he was considering marriage, he replied simply, "Yes, a fairer bride than any of you have ever seen."

Today, millions of people honor St. Francis for his devotion to "lady poverty." Celebrations differ from country to country and town to town. Sometimes bags with gold-colored rocks are placed before altars to represent the giving up of riches. Other times, people make light of wealth by using coins in their dances. Since St. Francis believed all living creatures were his friends, celebrations sometimes include animals.

Día de los Muertos

Boys and girls giggle behind masks:

Skulls
Devils
Ghosts

NOVEMBER

Pulling on strings brings sugary skeletons alive,
a boogaloo of be-bopping bones.

A loving celebration of the old ones.

NOVIEMBRE

Bonfires burn on curbs along the streets. Carved lanterns swing from trees, while inside cozy homes, the aroma of baking cakes and sugary breads swells from kitchens. Framed pictures of deceased loved ones dwell on offering tables. Flowers, candles, and gaily dressed toy skeletons crowd the handmade altars.

The bright lights and mouth-watering smells assist the spirits of dead relatives in finding their way home. Loving families celebrate their return with a fun-filled feast.

Local theaters honor the dead by putting on plays. Ghosts and eerie voices rise from tombs on stage. Chocolate "funeral processions" parade down streets, led by miniature hearses glistening with candied fruits. Even the tiny coffins look delicious. All the while, children beg their parents for puppet skeletons that dance on strings.

Día de Los Santos Inocentes

Beware little ones.
Pranksters wish to trick you.

"Swallow a camel," they say.
"Or be flattened by a gnat."

Do not be fooled!

DECEMBER

DICIEMBRE

On Mexico's April Fool's Day, think twice if a friend asks to borrow money. The loan could be repaid with a foolish toy or handwritten note:

Inocente palomita,
que te dejaste engañar,
sabiendo que en este día
nada se debe prestar.

Innocent little dove,
you have let yourself be fooled,
knowing that on this day,
you should lend nothing.

Be especially cautious if someone invites you to his or her house for supper. Steaming *sopapillas* or *empanaditas* might crown the serving platter. But on this day, odd things may lurk inside the puffy pastry—gobs of cotton or bitter flour. Being tricked by this type of prank makes an "innocent" of the gullible one.

January (Fiesta de San Antonio Abad):

Anthony the Great (c. 251–356) is an Egyptian Christian saint known for a life of self-denial and discipline. Following other Christians who practiced isolation, St. Anthony ventured into the alkaline desert west of the Nile. According to legend, his only companions during his thirteen years of self-exile were animals. In many parts of the world, a Blessing of the Animals ceremony takes place on the Feast of St. Anthony, commonly celebrated on January 17th.

February (Wine Harvest):

Many communities along the southern coast of Peru celebrate the pruning of grapevines *(poda)* in July. The pressing or stomping of grapes *(pisa)* follows harvest in late February. On larger vineyards, the operation of mechanized equipment has caused such festivities to be discontinued. In small vineyards, however, the tradition lives on.

March (Corn-Planting Ceremony):

The Quiché Indians of Guatemala are the largest of all ethnic groups speaking a Maya language. Their pre-Columbian ancestors understood the importance of bountiful crops of corn. Today, as in earlier times, the domesticated cereal grain appears at every meal and is put to many other uses in everyday life.

In the small, stucco-white town of Chichicastenango, which lies on the crest of the Quiché Mountains, flower petals are scattered on the floor at a special mass the Sunday before planting. Later, families gather in the streets, creating intricate mosaics designed with colorful kernels of corn.

April (Sealing the Frost):

On April 8th, the Cuchumatán Indians of Santa Eulalia, Guatemala, follow holy men up a mountainside to a cliff. After a rope is looped around a prayer-maker's waist, he is lowered over a ledge beside the place where killing frost is believed to live. There he dangles precariously with a bucket of plaster or cement. He seals the crack with this mortar to make sure the frost won't escape and harm corn crops.

May (Cinco de Mayo):

The Battle of Puebla (May 5, 1862) took place during a chaotic time in Mexico's history. After the nation gained independence from Spain in a violent struggle (1821), followed by political takeovers and the Mexican-American War (1846–1848), the national economy dipped dangerously low. During this period, Mexico accumulated heavy debts to several European nations, including France. Napoleon III used the debt issue to try and establish French leadership in Mexico.

During the celebration of Cinco de Mayo, an actor plays General Zaragoza, leader of the Mexican army. An embroidered banner proclaiming ¡VIVA MÉXICO! swings from the brim of his hat. The actor portraying General Lorencez, head of the French army, wears ¡VIVA FRANCIA! *Chicancos* (guerilla forces) join soldiers in uniforms from mixed historical periods, streaming through the crowd. *Soldaderas* (women soldiers) follow the men, cooking for them and fighting at their sides. The dolls on their backs signify babies taken into battle by necessity.

June (Inti Raymi):

The center of the Inca empire was located in Cusco, high in the Andes Mountains in southern Peru. In the 1400s and early 1500s Incans gathered during the winter solstice to honor the sun in a ceremony that beckoned to the massive star to return and warm fertile fields.

Today Inti Raymi (Festival of the Sun) is one of the largest festivals in Cusco. It's also celebrated in other parts of Peru, throughout South America, and the world. The festival's centerpiece takes place on June 24, the actual day of Inti Raymi.

Indigenous Peruvian dishes steam from decorated tables: *escabeche* (fish either poached or fried, then marinated before serving) and *mazamorra* (a dessert similar to spoon pudding made with colorful corn, fruit and spices).

July (Pilgrimage of Saut d'Eau):

One of the most popular festivals in Haiti, Pilgrimage of Saut d'Eau (Waterfall), takes place in Ville Bonheur, a town sixty miles from the capital city of Port-au-Prince. Thousands of Haitians and foreign visitors make a pilgrimage to the waterfall where Erzulie Freda—the voodoo spirit of art and romance—is believed to have appeared twice in the nineteenth century.

Voodoo is a spiritual system of faith and rituals traditionally attributed to West Africa. The oral tradition of faith stories carries genealogy, history, and fables to subsequent generations. Although its core wisdom originated in Africa long before Europeans began the slave trade, the structure of voodoo, as known today, was born in Haiti during the European colonization.

August (Pilgrimage to Nuestra Señora de los Angeles Basilica):

During August, Costa Rica celebrates its patron saint, Nuestra Señora de los Angeles (Our Lady of Angels). While searching for firewood on August 2, 1635, a poor woman named Juana Pereira found a small image of the Virgin beside a footpath near Cartago, Costa Rica's capital until 1832.

Juana carried it home where it disappeared, only to be rediscovered at the same place. The statue repeated this behavior several times—being taken home, then to the parish church—each time returning to the site where Juana found it.

The locals believed Our Lady wanted them to build a shrine on the site. So they did. In 1935 Pope Pius XI declared the shrine of the Lady of Angels a basilica.

September (Águas de Oxalá):

In Salvador, Brazil, worshippers observe a rite of purification called Águas de Oxalá (Waters of Oxalá) on the last Friday of September. According to the Yoruba religion, Oxalá (also known as Obatala) dwells on the top of a mountain where he created all people. Because he drank too much palm wine while making one batch, people with birth defects fall under his protection.

The Yoruba people are a large ethno-linguistic group in Africa (predominantly in Nigeria) and in the Americas, which has influenced religions such as Candomblé, practiced chiefly in Brazil.

October (Fiesta de St. Francisco de Asís):

Saint Francis of Assisi, Italy (1181-1226) was a Roman Catholic who founded the order of Friars, commonly known as the Franciscans. Francis spent most of his childhood in the world of books, because his father's wealth afforded a privileged education. As an adult, Francis believed the average person should be able to pray in his own language. For this reason, he wrote his sermons in the dialect of Umbria instead of Latin.

Many stories about St. Francis revolve around his love of animals. According to one legend, he thanked his donkey from his deathbed for helping him throughout his life. His donkey is said to have wept. Since Francis is known as the patron saint of animals, birds, and the environment, Catholic churches customarily hold ceremonies honoring animals on the feast day of St. Francis, October 4.

November (Día de los Muertos):

Mexicans celebrate the ancient tradition of Day of the Dead during the first days of November. Long before Spain conquered Mexico, the native people believed the souls of those who passed away return once a year to visit their loved ones.

Today, families adorn offering tables with brightly colored cloths, platters of food, photographs, candles, and toys. The spirits of the dead use their supernatural sense of sight and smell to find their way home. Families celebrate their return with a festive banquet. During the meal everyone laughs at funny stories about the living and the dead and rattles off silly poems that poke fun at death.

When the clock chimes midnight the votive candles are snuffed out. It's time for the spirits to leave—that is, until next year's visit.

December (Día de Los Santos Inocentes):

Los Santos Inocentes (Day of the Innocent Saints) takes place on December 28th. In earlier times in Mexico, friends sent each other notes describing a personal tragedy that required money or a household item. If the friend forgot the day and assisted them, they later received a gift of sweets or small toys in memory of the Innocents lost to King Herod.

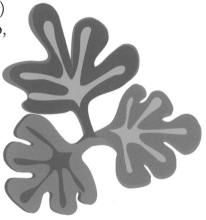

Although the roots of the holiday are violent—King Herod ordering his soldiers to seek out and murder all newborns in an effort to destroy the infant child god—in modern times, the practices are frivolous and similar to the U.S. version of April Fool's Day.

Pronunciation
Spanish names of the months

(January): Enero (eh-NEH-roh)

(February): Febrero (feh-BREH-roh)

(March): Marzo (MAHR-soh)

(April): Abril (ah-BREEL)

(May): Mayo (MAH-yoh)

(June): Junio (HOO-nyoh)

(July): Julio (HOO-lyoh)

(August): Agosto (ah-GOHS-toh)

(September): Septiembre (seh-TYEHM-breh)

(October): Octubre (ohk-TOO-breh)

(November): Noviembre (noh-BYEHM-breh)

(December): Deciembre (dee-SYEHM-breh)